The day the world turned upside down

By Mike Tibbetts

Dedicated to all who did their part.
Thank you from the bottom of my heart!

We woke one day to the world upside down.
A virus had come and overrun our small town.
The world as we knew it would soon be gone.
This is OUR story and the battle we won!

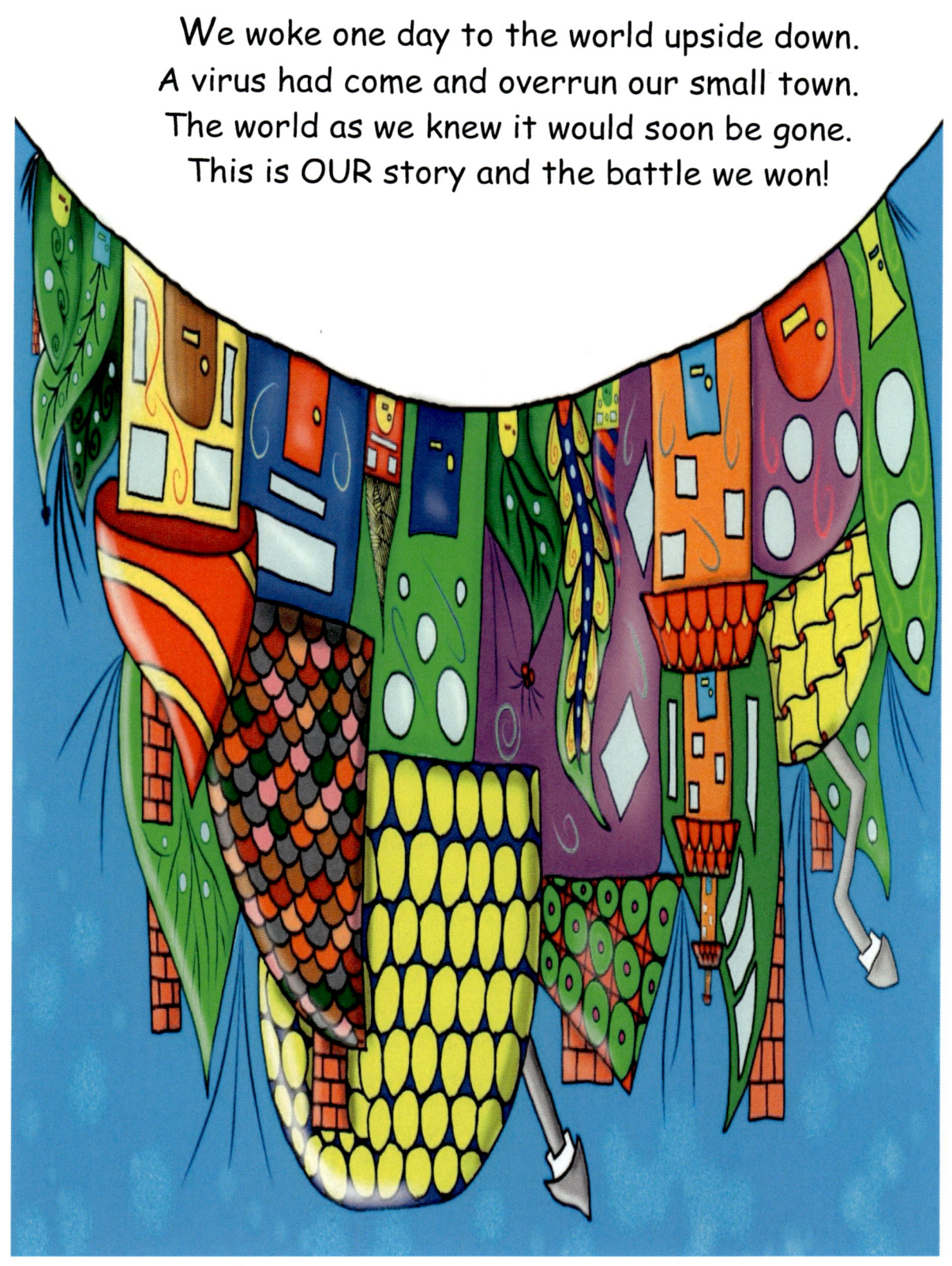

It started off bad, it created a panic.
Supplies ran out, it was mayhem and manic.
"COME ON!" people cried. "Let others get some.
We're in this together, this won't be fun."

The schools had no choice, the doors had to lock.
The teachers missed every last one of their flock.
Parents stepped up, with large shoes to fill,
This will be tough like rolling up hill.

No playing with friends or hanging out anymore.
No touching, no hugging that was the law!
No visits from grandma or grandpa today.
It was called social distancing, that was the way.

Restaurants were forced to shut their front doors.
Soon our small town was full of blank stores.
As all of their customers now stayed away.
But tomorrow brought hopes of a bright new day.

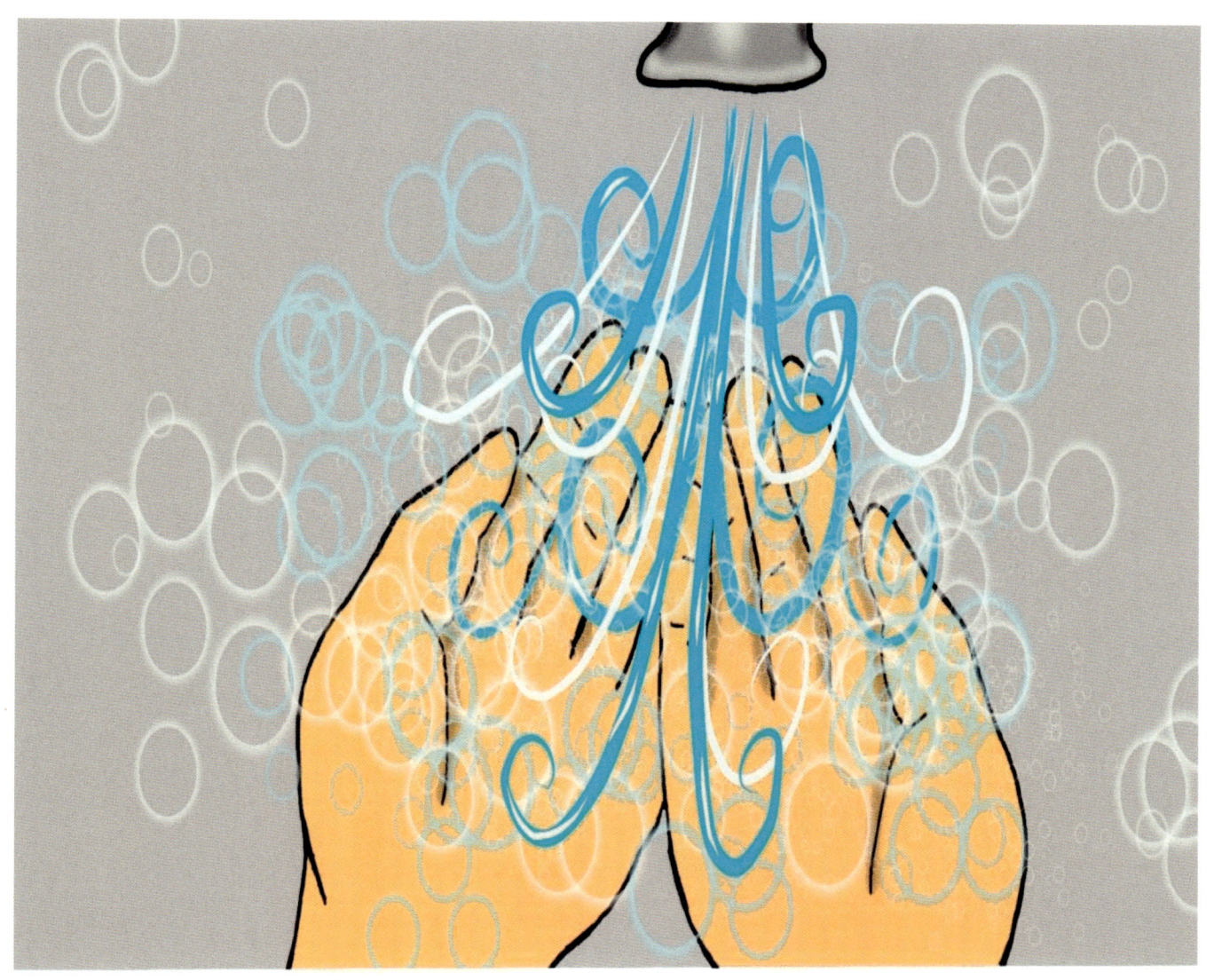

We fought without weapons and without guns.
Our only defense washing fingers and thumbs.
Doctors and nurses fought on the front line.
Stores provided food for your house and mine.

Teachers worked hard to teach kids through a screen.
This was now normal like in a dream.
Gym class was taught in our living room.
It kept us all healthy until life could resume.

People wrote messages of hope on their drive.
Like, WE CAN DO IT! And WE WILL SURVIVE!
Strangers smiled and waved on their walks.
Families connected using video to talk.

The earth was healing, and pollution subsided.
We were a species that wasn't divided.
Rivers ran clear and birds started to sing.
Warm weather was coming it would finally be spring

Work together is what we should do.
This won't be easy, I'll stand with you.
Love each other, it will be okay.
I can see light at the end of the day.

Made in the USA
Monee, IL
13 April 2020